Old Lobster Claws
Copyright © 2021 by Ian T Rowan

All rights reserved. No part of this publication may be reproduced, distributed, or transmitted in any form or by any means, including photocopying, recording, or other electronic or mechanical methods, without the prior written permission of the author, except in the case of brief quotations embodied in critical reviews and certain other non-commercial uses permitted by copyright law.

Tellwell Talent
www.tellwell.ca

ISBN
978-0-2288-5641-2 (Hardcover)
978-0-2288-5642-9 (Paperback)
978-0-2288-5640-5 (eBook)

'Twas right before Christmas,
when under the sea,
the Mussels were flexing
for what would soon be.

The Clams and the Oysters
were tucked in their beds
with visions of Mollusks
baked up in some bread.

As Angel Fish sang,
gathered round in a choir,
the Salmon stayed warm
by the fissures of fire.

The Dolphin and Shark,
both Flipper and Jaws,
anxiously waited
for Old Lobster Claws.

Seahorses came pulling
Old Claws in his sleigh
with presents in seashells,
Hip! Hip! Hooray!

The Cod, he did wonder,
"Now what is the matter?"
as his old friend the Flounder
flopped out of the batter.

The Octopus danced
with two arms and six legs,
serving up platefuls
of scrambled fish eggs.

On the iceberg the Penguins,
dressed up in their suits,
were wishing and hoping
he'd bring them new boots.

The Eel was electric!
It was really quite shocking!
He couldn't wait to see
what he'd get in his stocking.

Sea Corals adorned
with tinsel and holly
kept Old Lobster Claws
so happy and jolly.

While on top of the reef
fish were jumping with joy.
Oh, what will he bring us?
A Gull or a Buoy?

The waiting's now over.
We'd soon all be fed
with our presents delivered,
all snuggled in bed.

As Claws swam away
we could all hear him mutter,
"There's nothing to do
but add hot melted butter!"

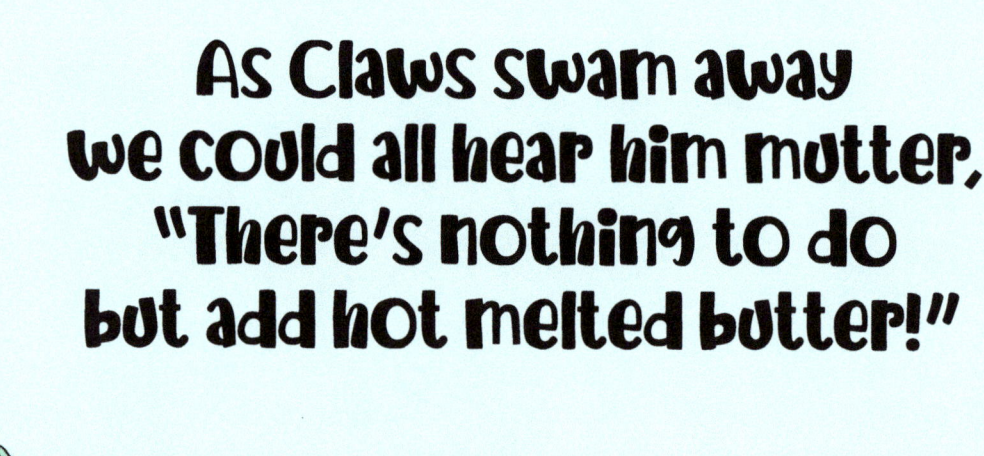

CPSIA information can be obtained
at www.ICGtesting.com
Printed in the USA
BVHW021119061221
623328BV00006B/508